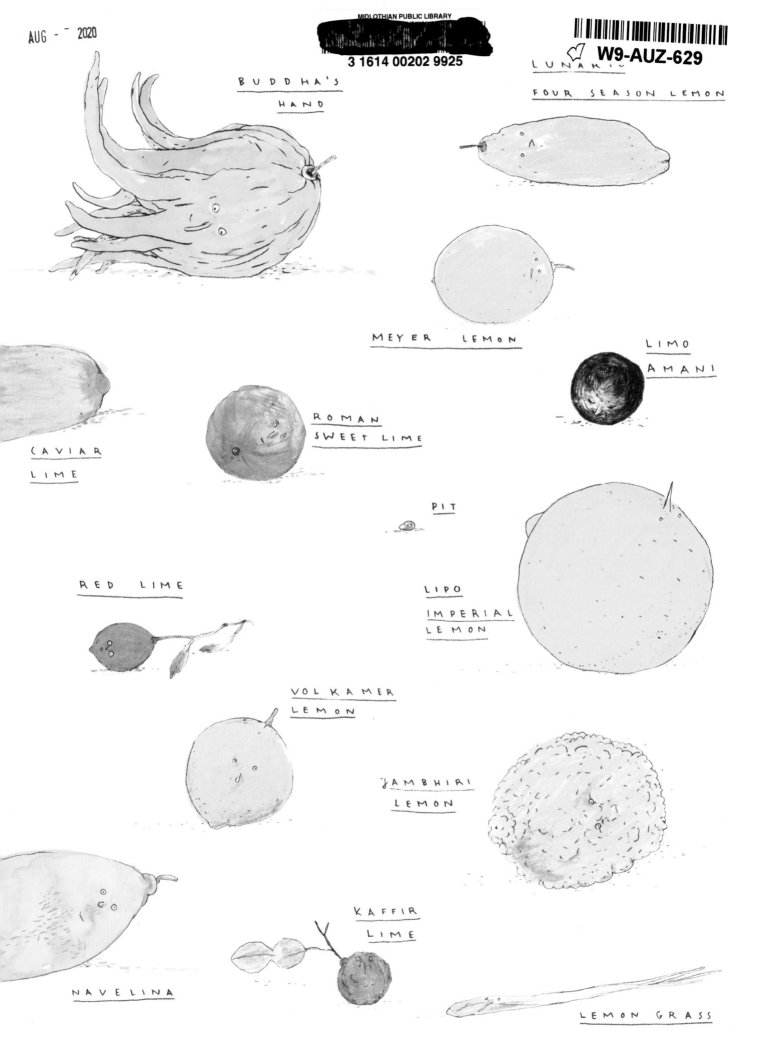

BUDDHA'S
HAND

LUNARIO
FOUR SEASON LEMON

MEYER LEMON

LIMO
AMANI

CAVIAR
LIME

ROMAN
SWEET LIME

PIT

RED LIME

LIDO
IMPERIAL
LEMON

VOLKAMER
LEMON

JAMBHIRI
LEMON

KAFFIR
LIME

NAVELINA

LEMON GRASS

Nele Brönner was born in Marburg/Lahn, Germany, and studied visual communications at the University of the Arts in Berlin. She is still living in Berlin, and works as an author and illustrator of children's books and comics. In 2015, she won the Serafina Prize for children's literature, and in 2019, she was awarded the Gold Medal of the Book Art Foundation.

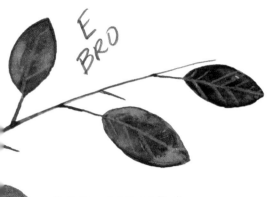

FOR WANJA

First published in the United States, Great Britain, Canada, Australia, and New Zealand in 2020
by NorthSouth Books Inc., an imprint of NordSüd Verlag AG, CH-8050, Zürich, Switzerland.

Distributed in the United States by NorthSouth Books Inc., New York, NY 10016.
Library of Congress Cataloging-in-Publication Data is available.
Printed by Livonia Print in Riga, Lettland
ISBN: 978-0-7358-4418-6
1 3 5 7 9 · 10 8 6 4 2

www.northsouth.com

NELE BRÖNNER

# LEMON CHILD

TRANSLATED BY DAVID HENRY WILSON

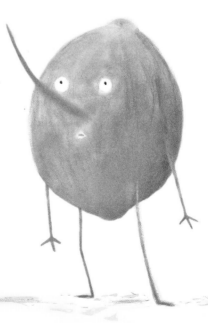

The lemon tree was proud of herself. This year was her best ever! She had never produced so many blossoms before, and now there were tiny lemons hanging from every branch. As soon as the sun shone, there was a wonderful atmosphere in the lemon tree. The little lemons chattered and giggled and sang silly songs.

All of them were happy, except one lemon child named Tony. It got on his nerves to see his brothers and sisters in such good moods just because they were turning yellow. They kept their round tummies exposed to the sun and swung merrily in the summer breeze. Tony preferred to stay in the shade.

HEE HEE

HEE HEE

His brothers and sisters had realized long ago that Tony was
a pretty miserable lemon and didn't like anything that they liked.
Tony tried to ignore them, but deep inside he was infuriated
when they made fun of him.

"They can get lost!" He wanted to stay exactly as he was:
emerald green and silky smooth.

YOU ARE GREEEEN.

WE'RE ALL YELLOW.
YOU'VE STAYED GREEN.
YOU'RE THE SILLIEST LEMON
I HAVE EVER SEEN.

The mild days passed, and one morning a very yellow lemon began to twist and turn, and then with a loud cry, jumped down from the tree.

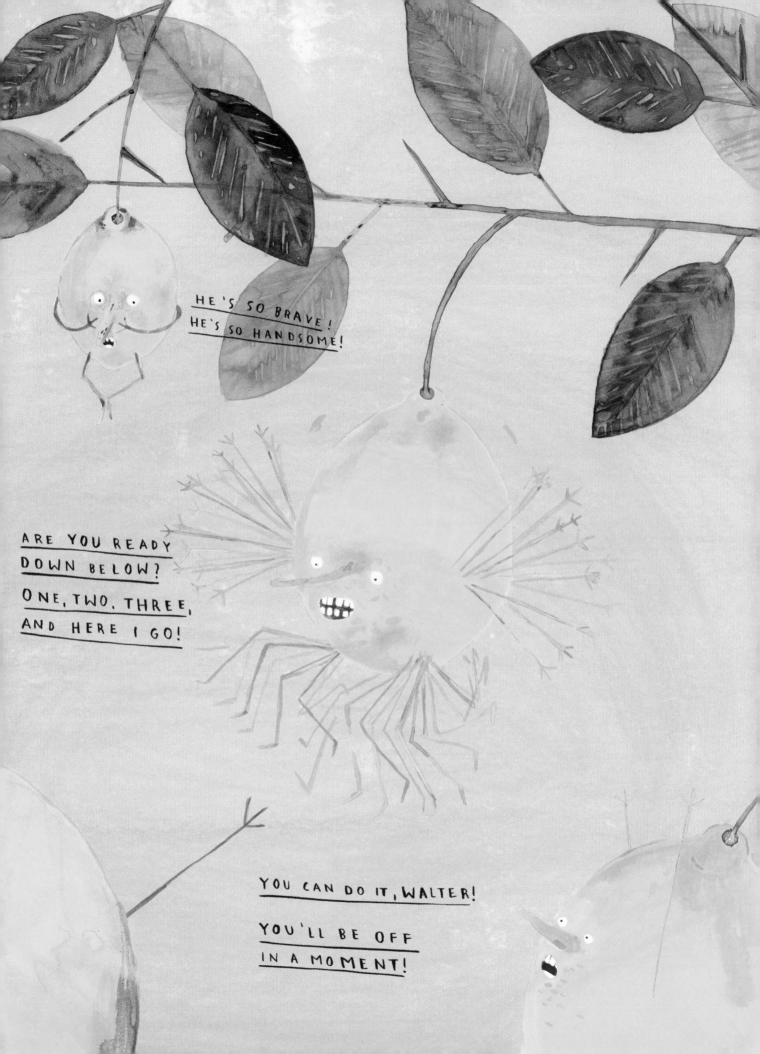

Now they all wanted to jump from the tree. All except Tony.
He refused to even practice twisting and turning. There was no
way he would ever jump.

It was not long before Tony was left all alone dangling from
the tree.

One day at noon, the monkey from the neighbor's garden visited the lemon tree.

"Well, Tony, what are you up to? Don't you want to jump down like the others and see the world?"

"I can see the world from up here. I'm green, and I'm going to keep hanging here—and no one's going to stop me," snapped Tony.

"Maybe you can see the garden, Tony," said the monkey, laughing, "but you can't see the world. The world is really big, and there are plenty of places for lemons to go to and plenty of things they can become."

"Really? So what else can lemons become?" asked Tony.

"Just about anything," replied the monkey. "Little sweets, ice cream, soap, or a big tree, just like your mother. Anything you'd like! I've seen the craziest things myself."

THERE'S A WHOLE WORLD WAITING
FOR YOU, LEMON CHILD.

The day turned to twilight.

"What's it like, Tony, being all alone up here?" asked the screech owl from a branch nearby.

"I've got peace and quiet at last," growled Tony. "I can have a good sleep, without all the others jumping around and getting on my nerves."

"You know, in the evening light you look a bit yellow. Very pretty," said the screech owl as she glided softly away.

That night, Tony felt a bit lonely in his tree. He thought about what the monkey had told him. Maybe it would be nice to go out into the world at last? He could also jump down if he wanted to. . . .

The porcupine came wandering through the long grass below. He raised his head high in the air and had a good sniff.

SO, LEMON CHILD, DO YOU WANT TO STAY UP THERE WAITING FOR SPRING?

Early the next morning, when the mist was still hanging over the fields,
Tony made his decision. He was going to practice moving around. First,
he twisted here, and then he turned there. Next, he did a cautious wiggle
and a careful waggle. And after that, he swung backward and forward,
farther and farther. There was a tickling in his tummy, and he swung higher
and higher, faster and faster. Suddenly, there was a cracking sound!

VRRROOOOOMM
VRRROOOOOMM

AHHHA!

AHHHA!

AHH!

WAAAH!

OUCH!

PLONK

As if from a powerful gust of autumn wind, and with a loud cry,
Tony jumped from the branch and down into the long grass.
*Wheeee!* But he landed flat on his back. Ouch!

For the first time, he looked up at the tree and beyond into the
wide sky. Perhaps it was true that the world was a lot bigger than
he had thought. The sky certainly was.

A fresh breeze blew through the garden, and a boy came skipping through the dry stalks. He looked up at the crown of the lemon tree, but there were no more lemons hanging from the branches. The boy searched through the green grass and between the roots.

"If I were yellow, he'd find me," Tony thought sadly, wiping a bitter tear from the corner of one eye. "The last lemon of the year—the boy would be so pleased."

Tony, the last lemon child, tried to make a rustling sound in the grass. It worked. It actually worked! The boy found him. He lifted Tony up and pressed him against his nose.

"A green lemon—they have the nicest smell of all," he said.

The boy carried Tony home with him.

"There we are, lovely lemon. I'll put you on my windowsill,"
said the boy, and made room among his treasures. "This is
a good place. You can lie here and look out at the world."
Tony smiled.

HI THERE!

MORNING!

MORNING!

MORNING!

CHEERS, MATE!

HELLO!

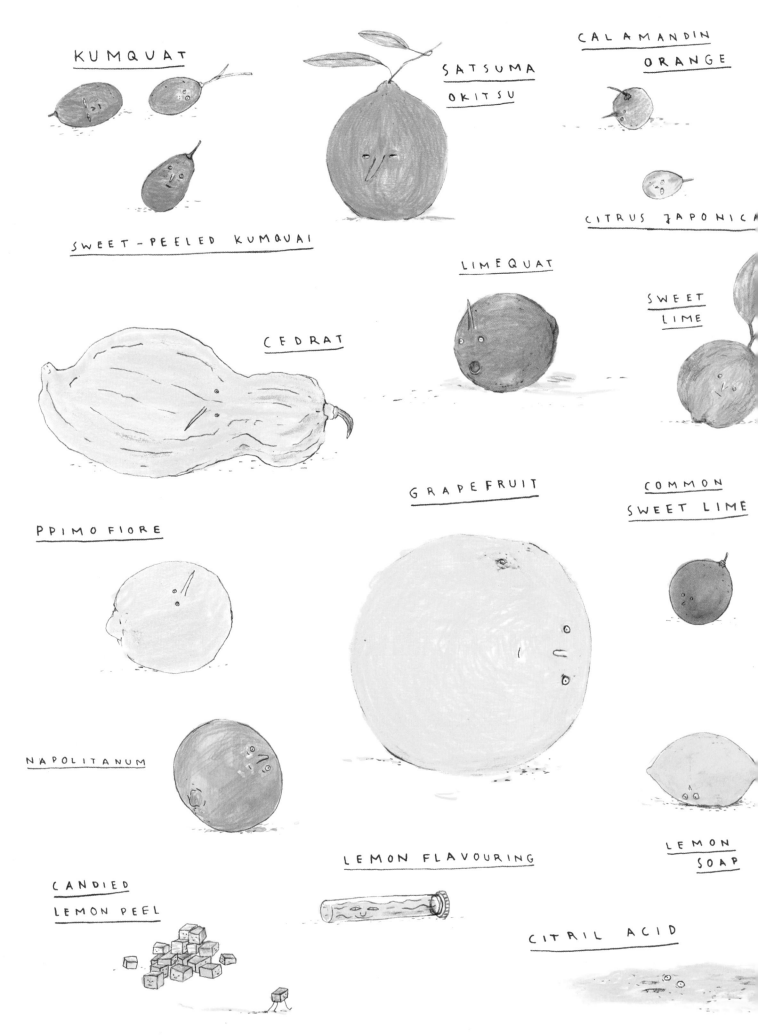

KUMQUAT

SATSUMA

OKITSU

CALAMANDIN

ORANGE

CITRUS JAPONICA

SWEET-PEELED KUMQUAI

LIMEQUAT

SWEET
LIME

CEDRAT

GRAPEFRUIT

COMMON
SWEET LIME

PPIMO FIORE

NAPOLITANUM

LEMON FLAVOURING

LEMON
SOAP

CANDIED
LEMON PEEL

CITRIL ACID